Dear Parent:
Your child's love of reading starts here!

Every child learns to read in a different way and at his or her own speed. Some go back and forth between reading levels and read favorite books again and again. Others read through each level in order. You can help your young reader improve and become more confident by encouraging his or her own interests and abilities. From books your child reads with you to the first books he or she reads alone, there are I Can Read Books for every stage of reading:

SHARED READING
Basic language, word repetition, and whimsical illustrations, ideal for sharing with your emergent reader

BEGINNING READING
Short sentences, familiar words, and simple concepts for children eager to read on their own

READING WITH HELP
Engaging stories, longer sentences, and language play for developing readers

READING ALONE
Complex plots, challenging vocabulary, and high-interest topics for the independent reader

ADVANCED READING
Short paragraphs, chapters, and exciting themes for the perfect bridge to chapter books

I Can Read Books have introduced children to the joy of reading since 1957. Featuring award-winning authors and illustrators and a fabulous cast of beloved characters, I Can Read Books set the standard for beginning readers.

A lifetime of discovery begins with the magical words "I Can Read!"

Visit www.icanread.com for information
on enriching your child's reading experience.

AaBbCc

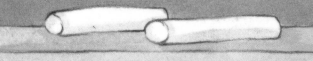
cat

For Rogan
—L.M.S.

For Phoebe
—S.K.H.

I Can Read Book® is a trademark of HarperCollins Publishers.

Library of Congress Cataloging-in-Publication Data is available.
ISBN 978-0-06-170224-2 (trade bdg.) — ISBN 978-0-06-170223-5 (pbk.)

15 16 17 18   PC/WOR 10 9 8 7 6 5 4 3   ❖   First Edition

Mittens
at School

story by **Lola M. Schaefer**
pictures by **Susan Kathleen Hartung**

HARPER
An Imprint of HarperCollins*Publishers*

Mittens is at school.

He will be Nick's show-and-tell.

"Sit here, Mittens," says Nick.
"Show-and-tell will be later."
Mittens watches Nick write.

Mittens watches Nick paint.

Mittens wants something to do.

"It's time for gym class,"
says Nick. "Wait here, Mittens.
We will be back soon."
Mittens sits and waits.

But he wants something to do.

Mittens runs to the math table.

Clink. Clink. Clink.

He pushes the counting beads.

CRASH!

The beads crash to the floor.

Mittens jumps down.

What can he do now?

Mittens runs to the piano.

Plink. Plink. Plink.

He walks across the keys.

SLAM!

The piano lid slams shut.

Mittens jumps down.

What can he do now?

Mittens runs to the bookcase.

He jumps up.

Flip. Flip. Flip.

He flips the pages of a book.

The class comes back.

BAM!

The book falls.

17

"Who dropped that book?"
asks the teacher.

Slowly, Mittens steps out.
"Meow."

"Who are you?"
asks the teacher.

"This is Mittens," says Nick.

"He's my show-and-tell."

"Hello, Mittens,"
says the teacher.
"Come meet our class."

At last,

Mittens has something to do!

Mittens is a good show-and-tell.

Purr. Purr.

cat